VIKING KESTREL

Distributed by the Penguin Group
27 Wrights Lane, London W8 5TZ, England
Viking Penguin Inc., 40 West 23rd Street, New York, New York 10010, USA
Penguin Books Australia Ltd, Ringwood, Victoria, Australia
Penguin Books Canada Ltd, 2801 John Street, Markham, Ontario, Canada L3R 1B4
Penguin Books (NZ) Ltd, 182–190 Wairau Road, Auckland 10, New Zealand

Penguin Books Ltd, Registered Offices: Harmondsworth, Middlesex, England

First American edition 1990

Typeset in Univers
Printed by L.E.G.O. Vicenza

ISBN 0–670–83075–5

Oh, no!

SARAH GARLAND

VIKING KESTREL

Getting dressed

Oh, no!

Washing face

Oh, no!

Off to Granny's

Oh, no!

Hello Granny

Oh, no!

13

Kissing Granny

Oh, no!

Getting lunch

Oh, no!

Eating lunch

Oh, no!

Clearing up

Oh, no!

Country walk

Oh, no!

Goodbye Granny

Oh, no!

Back home

Oh, no!

Be good

Good night